HELLO! WEL[COME] TO THE FABUMOUSE [WORLD OF THE] THEA SISTERS!

Hi, I'm Thea Stilton, Geronimo Stilton's sister! I am a special reporter for _The Rodent's Gazette_, the most famous newspaper on Mouse Island. I love traveling and meeting new mice all over the world, like the Thea Sisters. These five friends have helped me out with my adventures. Let me introduce you to these fabumouse young mice!

Colette has a real passion for fashion. She loves to design her own clothes in her favorite color, pink.

Violet loves studying and learning new things. She is a fan of classical music and dreams of becoming a famous violinist someday.

Pamela loves pizza so much she eats it for breakfast. She is a skilled mechanic who can fix just about any motor she gets her paws on.

PAULINA is shy and loves to read about faraway places. But she loves traveling to those places even more.

Nicky is from the Australian Outback, where she developed a love of nature and the environment. This outdoors-loving mouse is always on the move.

Thea Sisters

Thea Stilton

MOUSEFORD ACADEMY

THE SECRET INVENTION

Scholastic Inc.

ISBN 978-0-545-78904-2

Published by Scholastic Inc., 557 Broadway, New York, NY 10012. SCHOLASTIC and associated logos are trademarks and/or registered trademarks of Scholastic Inc.

Stilton is the name of a famous English cheese. It is a registered trademark of the Stilton Cheese Makers' Association. For more information, go to www.stiltoncheese.com.

Text by Thea Stilton
Original title *Il progetto super segreto*
Cover by Giuseppe Facciotto
Illustrations by Barbara Pellizzari and Francesco Castelli
Graphics by Marta Lorini

Special thanks to Joanne Ruelos Diaz
Translated by Julia Heim
Interior design by Becky James

12 11 10 9 8 7 6 5   18 19 20/0

Printed in the U.S.A.   40
First printing, January 2015

SECRET PASSWORD

The brilliant colors of AUTUMN filled the garden at Mouseford Academy. The red and gold leaves on the trees waved gently, moved by a light breeze. What a fabumouse day!

Professor Rosalyn Plié raised her snout and took a deep breath of the clean, fresh air. A nature walk was just what she needed to find inspiration for the dance class

choreography she was creating.

Suddenly a deep **rumble** blasted through the garden, **shaking** the tree branches and sending the fallen leaves swirling across the ground. Professor Plié looked up and saw a large **HeLiCoPteR** with the initials RF painted on the side. It was coming in for a landing!

"Looks like Ryder and Ruby are back from their vacation!" a voice said behind the professor.

A MELODIOUS voice chimed in, "Onboard their personal helicopter, of course. What a way to travel!"

The teacher turned to see *Nicky* and **Violet**, two students from her dance class, approaching.

The mice were carrying two enormouse **BOXES** across the garden.

"Hello, Professor!" they called.

Professor Plié waved and smiled sweetly. But the mice were headed toward Mouseford's GARAGE. They had their paws full and couldn't stop to chat. When they reached the door, Nicky put down her box and knocked.

"SECRET PASSWORD?" asked someone inside.

So heavy!

Nicky groaned. "Ugh! What a mouserific pain . . ."

But Violet replied confidently, "*Leonardo da Vinci!*"

And the door opened.

A NOT-SO-GRAND ENTRANCE

Meanwhile, the Flashyfurs' helicopter had landed in a field next to the academy. Ryder and Ruby got out, along with their mother, Rebecca. She had one last message for her children before they returned to school.

"Always remember that you two are winners," Rebecca instructed. "You were born to be in the spotlight!"

Ryder sighed and headed toward the academy without a word. But Ruby **smacked** a kiss on her mother's cheek. "Your motto is my motto, Mommy!"

Ruby walked after her brother, ready to follow her mother's words of wisdom immediately by making a triumphant entrance. She was wearing a beautiful *designer* outfit created just for her. She was sure that all her friends would shower her with attention, and she couldn't wait for her moment of glory!

"Here I am!" she announced, stopping in the doorway of the academy's main entrance. "You'll never guess what happened at the exclusive party we were invited to —"

Ruby's whiskers TWiTCHeD as soon as she realized no one was paying any attention to her!

"Hey! Am I invisible?!" Ruby sputtered, looking around. The hallways were swarming with students, but no one stopped to give Ruby more than a quick hello. They RUSHED by her, carrying boxes overflowing with strange equipment.

Even Ryder seemed confused by all the activity. "There must be something going on that we don't know about," he mumbled.

Just then, the brother and sister noticed a huge BOX OF PAWS coming straight toward them! It took them a moment to figure out it was actually Shen, carrying a giant box of equipment.

Ryder walked up to him. "Shen? Is that you back there? What's going on? It's like the academy has gone crazier than mice at an all-you-can-eat **cheese buffet**!"

Shen craned his neck from behind the box and saw his friend. "Wait, you don't remember? We're preparing for the big GAMS **competition** — the Global Alliance of Mice in Science! Professor Sparkle told us about it last month."

"Oh, yeah!" Ryder said, **SMACKING** his forehead. "I forgot."

Ruby just rolled her eyes. "Ugh. Science. What a **BORE**."

Shen ignored her and continued. "Tomorrow, groups of students from the most prestigious academies all over the

WORLD will arrive. They'll be here to present models of their science projects to a panel of famouse scientists. The best project wins MONEY so the team can make a real version!"

Suddenly, Shen had Ruby's attention. "So you're saying that this is some kind of competition . . . with a prize?" she asked.

"Exactly!" Shen said. "And we Mouseford students will have to WORK HARD to win!" Shen was so busy explaining the competition that he didn't notice motor OIL leaking out of his box and forming a dark puddle by his paws. "Sorry, I really have to get going," he said, starting to head off. "I need to organize the welcome for the other schools' delegates, arrange the award ceremony party, and — AAAH!"

Shen had slipped on the motor oil! His four paws went flying into the air.

THE MILKY WAY MICE

Shen fell hard on the ground, and the contents of the box **SPILLED** everywhere. Ryder bent down to help his friend . . . but Ruby scurried off in a flash. The only thing she was concerned about was not getting motor oil on her precious outfit!

A few minutes later, Ruby strutted into the LIZARD CLUBROOM, home of the club for girl mice at Mouseford. But when she saw that the room was EMPTY, she scowled. *How can I be in the spotlight when there's no audience?* she thought. She perked up when she heard a voice call her name: "Ruby!"

Finally! Ruby thought. She turned and struck a P©S:€ as Alicia came running over to greet her.

"YOU'RE BACK.!" Alicia squealed.

Ruby froze and her eyes **BULGED**. The head and paws of her friend were sticking out of a round costume covered with bizarre brownish stripes. She looked like an **ENORMOUSE BALL**!

And she wasn't alone. Connie and Zoe were right behind her, dressed the same way. The three of them clumsily squeezed around Ruby to say hello.

"Paws off my outfit!" Ruby hissed. "This is an exclusive design — though I can't say the same about your **horrible** outfits! What are you wearing?!"

"Well..." began Alicia. "They're costumes. We're dressed as **planets**!"

What are you wearing?!

"Professor Plié invited us to dance at the award ceremony for the science competition," Zoe explained. "We created a piece called '**The Milky Way Mice**'!"

Seeing the look of d*isapproval* on Ruby's face, Zoe jumped in. "The Thea Sisters are working on a science project. We didn't want to do a science project like them. They have to compete to win. We'll be performing in front of **everyone** no matter what."

"Unfortunately, there are **eIGHt**

planets and only **FOUR** of us," Alicia chirped. "So we were thinking of choosing—"

"Four?" Ruby interrupted. "What are you talking about? There are only three of you!"

"Yes, but we made a **COSTUME** for you, too!" Connie said. "We're Mars, Jupiter, and Saturn — and we saved the best role for you! You'll be the **SUN**!"

Alicia ran over to a box on the floor and took out a round costume covered in gold sequins. It had a zipper on one side and four holes for arms and legs.

Ruby gasped. "You can't possibly think that I would put on

such a **monstrosity**!" she cried.

"But it's for our dance number," Alicia muttered. "We're all supposed to orbit around you, and . . ."

"Enough!" Ruby squeaked. "Forget this dance business and come to my room. We have **important** things to think about. I want to know every last detail about what the Thea Sisters have been up to while I was away."

TiME TO
EXPERiMENT

Over in the Mouseford garage, the Thea Sisters were hard at work. They had set up their gear in the handymouse's **workshop**. It was one of Pamela's favorite places on campus, and was the perfect spot to work on their Global Alliance of Mice in Science project.

Pam was stretched out underneath a **strange armchair** with wheels.

"That's it!" **Pam** cried

happily as she slid out from under the chair. She got up on her GREASE-COVERED paws, but didn't mind one bit. She was right at home surrounded by the NUTS AND BOLTS in the workshop. "This baby is ready for its first steps."

"I can't believe it!" Nicky said excitedly. "After weeks of work, the **MOUSEPOD 3000** is complete!"

The Mousepod 3000 was the girls' nickname for their invention. It was a **remote-controlled** chair that could move over any kind of terrain. It could even jump over obstacles!

"What do you mean, *complete*?" Colette objected as she sewed a piece of colorful fabric. "We certainly can't present it without a touch of flair."

"Well, we need to hurry with the lining,

mouselets," said PAULINA quietly. "The big judging day is tomorrow!"

"And we told the headmaster we would organize the welcome party for the other schools, too. We just haven't had the time!" Colette sighed.

But **Violet** wasn't concerned. "Don't worry, we'll figure it out," she said with a reassuring SMiLe.

Just then, someone knocked on the door:

"That must be Shen!" said Paulina. "Just in time!"

Pam nodded enthusiastically. "Shen's technical support was really valuable. He should take the first turn on the Mousepod 3000!"

The girls were about to ask for the secret password when the DOOR opened and their singing teacher, Professor Aria, appeared. Shen was leaning on her for support, his tail drooping behind him.

"I've brought your friend," Professor Aria explained, gesturing to Shen's foot. "He needed some help walking over from

the **INFIRMARY**." Professor Aria glanced around the workshop and added, "I must confess, I was **curious** to see your project, too!"

Paulina quickly scurried over to help Shen into a chair.

"Oh! What happened?" Paulina asked, pointing to the **BANDAGE** on Shen's foot with concern.

"I **sprained** my ankle . . ." Shen said sadly.

Pam's eyes lit up. "Fabumouse! Just what we need!"

The mice all turned to look at her in **SURPRISE**.

"Um . . . I mean . . . I'm very sorry that you're hurt," Pam explained. "But this way we can show how **useful** our invention is — it can help someone who can't walk!"

Shen's face brightened. "Is that true, Pam? Do you still think I can **HELP**?"

"Of course!" she replied. "The internal controls aren't working yet, so we'll guide you from Paulina's laptop. Put on the helmet and buckle your seat belt — **and we're off**!"

THE AMAZING MOUSEPOD 3000!

Shen made sure his helmet was secure, settled into the **CONTRAPTION**, and buckled the double seat belt. Next, the Thea Sisters surrounded him with **pillows**. As soon as he was comfortable, Paulina pushed a button on the computer, and the Mousepod 3000 started to rumble and shake.

WHIRRRRRRR!

The two front **wheels** lowered, the hood slid forward, and the whole vehicle closed up like an egg. Finally, the wheels began to turn and the Mousepod 3000 started to ZIGZAG around the floor!

"It's moving! It's moving!" Pam shouted. Nicky and Colette were standing closest to the exit. "Quick!" Pam called to them. "Open the door! I can't wait to try this thing outside!"

Paulina's paws flew as she worked the controls on her L A P T O P and directed the Mousepod 3000 out the open door. The small vehicle ventured onto the academy's paved road, with the Thea Sisters jogging close behind. Seeing their invention working perfectly was more exciting than bottomless mozzarella milkshakes!

"Let's try it on gravel!" Pamela urged Paulina. "Let's see how it does on a rocky road!"

"YOU GOT IT!" Paulina grinned and sent the Mousepod 3000 down a gravel path.

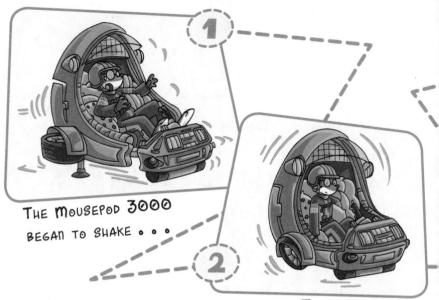

THE MOUSEPOD 3000
BEGAN TO SHAKE . . .

. . . THE WHEELS
LOWERED, AND THE PASSENGER
SEAT CLOSED . . .

BUMP BUMP BUMP!

The Mousepod 3000 BOUNCED over the stones like a kangaroo and started speeding toward a brick **WALL**. Oh no! The Thea Sisters had to do something — and fast! Otherwise, the Mousepod 3000

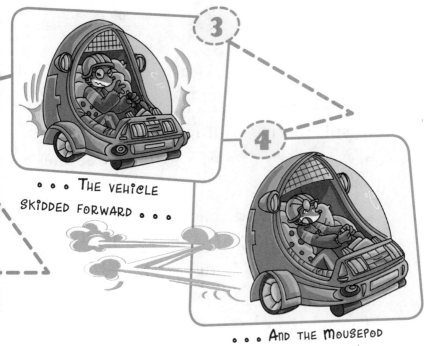

... THE VEHICLE SKIDDED FORWARD ...

... AND THE MOUSEPOD 3000 TOOK OFF!

could **crash** and **CRUMBLE** like grated Parmesan!

Pam shouted in alarm, "Paulina, engage the **propeller**!"

Paulina sprang into action like a mouse eating Muenster. She reached for the remote right away, and pressed down on a large, red button. But for a moment, the vehicle continued LURCHING forward — it was still heading right for the wall! Just in time, a spiral-shaped sail popped out of the top . . .

. . . and the Mousepod 3000 LIFTED into the air and cruised smoothly over the wall.

"**HOORAY!**" shouted Pam.

The others joined in, filled with pride and relief. What a **close call**! "Yay! Hooray! We did it!"

Paulina wiped her forehead. "I was worried for a second there — but look at it go!"

"That's truly mousetastic," Professor Aria exclaimed incredulously. "Your project . . . flies!"

Just then, the Mousepod 3000 tilted in the air and landed on its side with an enormouse **THUD**. Holey cheese!

The friends scurried over to the vehicle as fast as their paws would carry them. Luckily, Shen climbed out of the chair's cockpit. He was a bit dazed, but safe and sound. Whew!

"Don't worry, Shen," Pam said cheerily. "We'll fix those controls. I promise that tomorrow we won't have the same problems with the landing."

Shen just straightened his glasses and smiled. "That was the **MOST FUN EVER**! The Mousepod 3000 is truly fabumouse."

What a blast!

RUBY'S PLANS

Ruby's room, meanwhile, was feeling more like an **interrogation** zone. Ruby wanted to know everything about the Thea Sisters' project, but her friends didn't have enough information to satisfy her.

"They've been keeping their experiment a secret," Connie tried to explain. "All I've heard is that it's some kind of car for the **FUTURE**."

"And we'll know everything tomorrow anyway, right?" Alicia added, wiggling her whiskers.

"*Tomorrow?* What do you mean?" Ruby demanded.

"The judging is tomorrow," said Zoe.

"Each school can enter only two projects into the competition," Zoe continued. "So a panel of our professors is going to choose which Mouseford projects will represent the academy at the big competition —"

"And the Thea Sisters' idea is by far the favorite!" Alicia blurted out.

Ruby's snout wrinkled with annoyance. Her rivals would receive their millionth award, while she would be left standing alone like a ball of moldy mozzarella.

"What does it matter, anyway?" Zoe said, trying to calm her friend. "We don't even want to do a science project."

"Of course not," Ruby scoffed. "The only thing I need to know about science is HOW TO BUY the latest high-tech device."

That gave Ruby an idea! But she needed

to be by herself to make it happen . . .

"I'm tired! I need to relax!" she said, gesturing for her friends to leave. As soon as they went, she pulled out her **cell phone** — the most advanced model, of course. "Hi, Mommy. I need a favor. And I need it right **now**!"

Hi, Mommy.

ONE MYSTERIOUS MOUSE

The next morning, Nicky was up early for her **DAILY RUN**. The judging was later that day, and she was eager to **calm her nerves** with a good workout. On her way to the docks, she ran into **PROFESSOR PLOTFUR**, the drama teacher of the Fine Arts department. He was wearing a tracksuit and taking deep breaths of the crisp autumn air through his snout.

"Hello, Professor!" Nicky called. She ran over to her teacher and started jogging in place. "You must enjoy going for a **RUN** first thing in the morning, too," she said brightly.

Professor Plotfur turned in surprise.

"Um . . . of course!" he replied, rubbing his ear nervously. He had actually planned on a leisurely stroll, but he didn't want to seem lazy in front of a student. "I run . . . five miles . . . every morning . . ."

Huff . . . puff . . . pant!

"That's great!" Nicky said. "We can run together!"

The professor had no choice but to follow Nicky as she ZIPPED up the narrow dirt paths that led from the academy to the countryside. He was able to keep up for the first mile, but soon enough, it was taking every last bit of energy not to show Nicky how **tired** he was.

"Everything okay, Professor? Should we slow down?" Nicky asked.

"No . . ." he puffed. "I'm just . . ." he **panted**. "Getting warmed up . . ." he gasped.

At the third mile, he stopped and sat on a rock. "I was . . . suddenly inspired to write a new play . . ." he explained, trying to catch his breath. "You go on ahead," he continued with an **exhausted** wave of his paw.

Nicky handed the professor her water bottle and left him on the rock, wiping his sweaty brow. Then she SCAMPERED off to finish her run. Once she reached the village, she headed to the fisherman's DOCK to get a drink from the water fountain.

She was just about to head back to the school when she saw an agitated mouse getting off the ferry. She watched as he barked orders at the dockmice who

Watch out! That's fragile!

were taking boxes off the ferry and loading them into a small red van.

"BE CAREFUL!" he shouted. "Don't shake that! It's your tail on the line if something breaks!"

Wow, Nicky thought. *That mouse is wound up tighter than a mousetrap spring!* Then she glanced at her watch and jumped. It was already eight o'clock! If she didn't hurry, she would miss the presentation of the Mousepod 3000!

AN UNEXPECTED ENTRY

Nicky raced back to the academy at top speed. Once there, she ran straight to her room and took a quick shower. In minutes, she was heading for the **GYM**, where the science projects were being presented.

But right before she arrived, she saw Ruby, having a *HEATED ARGUMENT* with . . . the mouse from the dock! *He must have driven here in that red van,* Nicky speculated.

I want it NOW!

Nicky *crept* a little closer, curious to find out more. Who was this mysterious mouse, and why would he be arguing with Ruby?

Ruby sniffed and quickly *sensed* that she was being watched. She immediately moved away from her unknown companion and gave Nicky a friendly wave of her paw. "Hi, darling!" she drawled. "What are you doing out here? The **presentation** of science projects has already started."

Nicky was *suspicious*, but Ruby had a point. She was late! She gave Ruby a quick nod, then hurried off to find her friends.

"There you are!" Pam said, greeting her at the gym entrance and tugging her arm. "**Finally** — come on!"

Pam and Nicky headed over to the Mousepod 3000. Colette and Violet were making some final adjustments to the seat coverings they had worked **all night** to complete. They knew that no detail was too small to make a difference. Nearby, Shen buckled his protective **helmet**. They were just about ready!

Within minutes, the judging panel arrived and the mice presented the Mousepod 3000. The vehicle's performance was flawless! It **glided** along a line on the floor without swerving an inch. When it reached an obstacle, the spiral-shaped sail flew out and the **motorized** armchair jumped right over whatever was in its path. After a few feet, the Mousepod 3000 rolled to a gentle stop. A moment later, Shen stepped out and took a bow before the committee.

The judges had now seen all of the projects. Soon, they were ready to reveal the two projects moving ahead in the competition! Headmaster de Mousus was about to announce Mouseford's finalists when . . .

"Wait! You need to see my project, too!"

Here's MY project!

Everyone turned to see Ruby wheeling a HUGE TUB full of water with a small floating garden in the middle of it.

"This is a project that I've worked on all by myself for a very long time," Ruby announced. She was wearing a strange, FUTURISTIC headband and a forest-green coat. "It's an island that moves . . . that is, water currents move it to, um —" She paused and gave her headband a nudge. "Um, yes. So, it uses windmills . . . and solar panels . . . to produce fruit and WHat?! I can't hear!"

Ruby stopped, and a red flush covered her snout faster than a hungry cat after a mouse. "Oh, yes! It grows things to eat without needing fertilizer, while also minimizing pollution," she finished quickly.

While her presentation had been confusing,

Ruby's model was truly impressive. It was just like a real island. Waves lapped up on the shore.

Beautiful red **strawberries** grew in the miniature garden. Small generators even powered tiny fans that looked like windmills to create a gentle island breeze.

The professors on the judging committee whispered together. After a few minutes, they announced their decision. Mouseford Academy's submissions for the GAMS competition would be . . . the Mousepod 3000 and the miniature island!

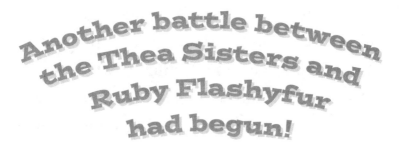

Another battle between the Thea Sisters and Ruby Flashyfur had begun!

WELCOME TO MOUSEFORD!

Once the science projects had been chosen, the Mouseford mice went down to the docks to **WELCOME** the other academies. Everyone wanted to make a good impression! Professors and students from prestigious schools all over the world were coming to participate.

As part of the welcoming committee, Violet and Colette were **DEDICATED** to making the visitors feel at home. Violet distributed **MAPS** of the island and information packets to each student, and Colette handed out **gift baskets** filled with local fruits and cheeses.

The other Thea Sisters took turns **hugging** their friends from the Yoshimune Academy in Japan, and trying to be pleasant to the snooty Ratridge Academy mice from England. Soon enough, the teams from the Mousesala Academy in India, the Mousekapov Academy in Russia, and the Snoutshire Academy in Scotland had arrived, too.

Delicious!

Meanwhile, Colette and Violet had their
PAWS FULL. The Snoutshire team seemed
like they hadn't eaten in months and were
gobbling up all the cheese from their gift
baskets. Steps away, Violet had to chase the
Russian team, who kept accidentally taking
the wrong bags and wandering off in the
wrong direction. The next few days were
definitely going to be **interesting**!

Wait! Stop!
It's this way!

RoBomoLE missing in Action!

The following day, the SUN was just creeping up over the horizon when the students from Mousekapov Academy banged on Violet's door.

"We have a **DISASTER**!" they shouted. "You have to help us!"

Violet dragged herself out of bed, rubbing her eyes, and opened the door. "**HUH?** What's going on? Is everything okay?"

"No, it's not okay at all! We've lost **Valentina**!" the mice yelped.

Violet rubbed her eyes. "Valentina? Is that one of your friends? She's probably just at breakfast . . ."

"No!" insisted Vladimouse, the **CAPTAIN** of the Mousekapov team. "Valentina only eats soil!" He looked horribly distraught.

Violet shook her snout quickly to wake herself up. *Am I dreaming?* she wondered.

"Valentina is our robot for the big competition!" explained Irina, another team member. "She's a **robotic mole** that locates water. She finds natural springs **underground**! We've been working on her for months, and now she's missing!"

The Mousekapov Academy students were **heartbroken**. They couldn't compete without their **project**! Violet desperately wanted to help them, but how? Then she remembered her Grandpa Chen's time-tested advice: "If you need to solve a problem, first drink a **cup of tea**."

Violet had the Mousekapov students sit down while she boiled water and handed out some cups. Her calmness relaxed the team a bit, and after some chamomile tea, they were able to explain how their robot was programmed to find water.

"She could be a very useful project, but **who knows** where she is now . . ." Irina trailed off sadly.

Violet snapped her fingers. "I have an idea!"

The team members all turned to look at her expectantly. "**WHaT?**"

"If we need to find Valentina . . . and Valentina is looking for **water** . . . we'll look for water . . . and we'll find Valentina!"

"That's a **FABUMOUSE** idea!" the Mousekapov students shouted. They leaped to their paws, eager to get started right away.

However, their simple plan turned out to be even harder than a stale wedge of **CHEDDAR** . . .

That's a fabumouse idea!

TROUBLE WiTH RATRiDGE

While Violet helped the Mousekapov students, everyone else was setting up in the big gymnasium. Each team had a specific area to DISPLAY ITS MODEL. Most of the groups had started to set up and Pamela, Paulina, Nicky, and Shen were already in position next to the Mousepod 3000.

Colette, on the other paw, was **stuck** with the team from Ratridge. The **snobby** students insisted on examining the space assigned to them before they would reveal their model. "We really have to display our project here where everyone can see?" they asked, **wrinkling** their snouts.

"The **RULES** are the same for everyone," Colette replied patiently.

"What about security?" asked their team leader, Sloane.

"What if someone copies our design?" Axel, another Ratridge team member, asked accusingly.

Our project is special!

"If you don't want to show your project, cover it up!" Colette blurted out, exasperated.

"That's not enough!" Sloane insisted. "We want a security mouse to stand guard at all times."

The Ratridge team was being completely unreasonable!

Colette was feeling frustrated from **head to tail** when Nicky rushed over to try and help. "I don't think you have anything to worry about. The presentations are about to begin. How could anyone have time to COPY you?" Nicky asked.

Groan...

Sloane sniffed. "Our model isn't like your **simplesnouted** little project. Our idea is **RE-VO-LU-TION-ARY**!"

Cheese and crackers, what a bunch of snooty mice! Colette and Nicky were so busy dealing with the Ratridge team that they didn't even notice when Violet entered the gym with the Mousekapov team right on her tail. Violet needed Pam and Shen's **help** finding Valentina the robomole before the judging began. There was no time to waste!

A few minutes later, Pam and Shen went off with Violet and Team Mousekapov. Ruby **noticed** from her project area, where she stood with Connie, Alicia, and Zoe. She raised an eyebrow.

Hmmm...

Suddenly, Ryder appeared and handed her a CD. "Mom told me to give this to you," he said with disinterest.

Ruby **snatched** the CD from her brother's paw. "Finally! Where is she? Why did she give it to you?" Her beady eyes darted around the gymnasium.

Ryder looked at his sister **suspiciously**. "She said that she needed to chat with the judges."

Ryder knew something was going on, and he didn't like the SMELL of it. "What are you two planning, Ruby?" he asked.

But his sister didn't reply. She was too busy KEEPING TABS on the Thea Sisters. Participating in the contest wasn't enough. Ruby wanted her island to win — but she also wanted the Mousepod 3000 to CRUMBLE like feta!

RUNAWAY
ROBOMOLE!

Over at the Mousepod 3000, Paulina was shocked by the demands of the Ratridge team. She stepped *CLOSER AND CLOSER* to Colette and Nicky to listen, leaving her computer **UNATTENDED** on the table.

Ruby knew this was her only chance to get the Thea Sisters *out of the game*. She snuck over, clutching the CD from her mother. With Paulina's back turned, she inserted the CD into Paulina's computer. A few seconds later, her paw was ready to eject it, when —

"Hi, Ruby! Do you need something?" Paulina asked.

"N-no, nothing!" Ruby stuttered. "Um, nice computer. Is it **new**?"

Before Paulina could answer, a **BIG CRASH** came from outside, followed by the thundering voice of Boomer, the academy's gardener and **HANDYMOUSE**. "Stop digging up my garden!" he yelled.

He'd found Valentina! Somehow the power button on the robomole had gotten stuck in the ON position, and the robot had made its way to Boomer's garden — with **DISASTROUS** results!

"Stop! Stop!" the gardener squeaked, chasing after the robomole in vain.

"Wow, she's **FAST**!" Nicky observed, jogging over to Violet and the Mousekapov students.

"Sooner or later the battery will die and she'll stop . . . **right**?" Violet asked hopefully.

Vladimouse wrung his paws and shook his head. "She recharges by swallowing

soil. And there's plenty of **dirt** here!" He gulped.

Violet thought for a moment. "I've got it! We need a **TRAP**!"

She grabbed a watering can and poured a **trail** of water from the garden to the entrance of the gym. "Get ready to grab her as soon as she comes out of the ground!" she directed.

But once again, it was easier said than done. Valentina burst out of the ground and jumped right onto Violet, *SENDING HER FLYING*.

The speedy robomole continued hustling toward the school entrance following the water, but when she got to the open door, she stopped and sniffed the air.

SNIFF SNIFF SNIFF

"We need more water!" cried the Mousekapov students. But it was too late. **Valentina** had already spotted some — the tank holding Ruby's island!

As the crowds rushed back into the school, Valentina ran over to the tank and dove in. SPLASH!!!

Oh no!

Before anyone knew what was happening, the **stranger** Nicky had seen at the dock **scooped** up the mole with a net, saving Ruby's project from destruction.

Nicky was shocked. "Him **AGAIN**?" But before she could talk to him, he **disappeared**!

Him again?

OUT OF
CONTROL!

The gymnasium was bustling. Before the stranger scurried away, he had **tossed** the robomole to Vlad, who switched it off. He and his teammates swarmed Violet and kept thanking her for her help, while the students from all the other schools **SCAMPERED** around, telling one another all about what they'd seen. They could hardly believe their eyes!

Little did everyone know that the excitement was just **beginning**!

The Thea Sisters' Mousepod 3000, which was connected to Paulina's computer, suddenly flashed a **green light** and buzzed to life.

The vehicle's **shell** closed up and it started to move — without anyone controlling it!

"The Mousepod 3000!" Pam squealed.

The Thea Sisters ran after the vehicle in confusion.

"Who's steering it?" Shen asked in disbelief.

"No one!" Paulina shouted, running to her computer. While the others darted after the vehicle, which was driving wildly around the gym, Paulina tapped the keys on her computer. But something was very wrong. The computer wasn't responding!

Bam! The Mousepod 3000 **smashed** into the Mousesala Academy booth, sending their spider-shaped peelers everywhere. What a mousetastic mess! Next, it zoomed out the door. Before the Thea Sisters knew what was happening, their project was heading toward a **CLIFF** at top speed . . . and there was nothing they could do to stop it!

"Wait!" Pam cried.

Violet waved her paws in the air. "Come back!"

"Stop! Where are you going? No! **NOT THAT WAY!**" Shen shouted desperately.

He couldn't help but cover his eyes with his paws as the Mousepod 3000 sped over the edge of the cliff and disappeared from sight.

Rumble . . . Rumble . . . Crunch!

"Nooo!" the Thea Sisters and Shen cried in despair. They couldn't believe it. Their creation had driven right **OFF A CLIFF**!

SOFTWARE SABOTAGE!

The whole Mousepod 3000 team was **speechless**. They returned to the gym with their snouts hung low and their tails between their legs. They sat down sadly at their empty booth.

Crowds of teachers and students gathered around the Thea Sisters to try to console them.

"I'm so sorry," Professor Aria said to them. "It really was such a useful project . . ."

Not wanting to stand out, even Ruby went over to offer her sympathy. But secretly, feeling bad for the Thea Sisters was the last thing on her mind. Her plan had worked out perfectly! After all, she was the one controlling the Mousepod 3000 through **SOFTWARE** she had uploaded from the CD.

And yet, she wasn't satisfied. The Thea Sisters **still** had everyone's attention!

"We can **CARRY** the vehicle back up," said the burly students from Snoutshire.

"We can help **REBUILD** it," the students from Yoshimune suggested, ready

We can help!

to offer their time and even their own tools.

Even the snobby mice from Ratridge had some kind words to say. "It was a good project. Ours is better, but we would have enjoyed beating you."

Ridiculous!

Ruby snorted. "Their rivals are trying to help them? RIDICULOUS! They should be happy that the Thea Sisters are **out of the competition**!"

But the support from the other teams actually made Pamela and her friends feel better. Even Shen perked up. "They're right! We can FIX the Mousepod 3000. It's not over yet!"

Paulina's ears tingled and she smiled wide. "We might not be able to fix it for this competition. But maybe we'll find out what went wrong . . ."

"And we'll win the next competition!" Nicky concluded, picking up a **WRENCH** and handing it to Pam.

Pam hesitated for a moment, but then she grabbed the wrench. "That's right, **SISTERS**! We may be down, but we're not out yet. Let's go get our Mousepod 3000!"

Pam and Nicky led a group of volunteers to retrieve their **INVENTION**. Even though some bushes had broken its fall and prevented major damage, it was still too **BROKEN** to compete.

Pam and Nicky went back to the gym to deliver the news and discovered something even **WORSE**. While the others were outside, Paulina and Shen had analyzed the **computer** for errors in the program.

"Hey! What's this?" Paulina asked, ejecting a disc from her laptop. "This wasn't in my computer this morning!"

Shen examined the disc. "This caused a **VIRUS** to send the wrong commands to the Mousepod 3000!"

Nicky looked at Pam. They were both thinking the same thing: **SOMEBODY WANTED THEM OUT OF THE COMPETITION!**

ON THE HUNT

"I can't believe **another student** could do this," Violet whispered. "It seems so complicated and underpawed. How would a student even know where to start?"

"Hey . . ." Nicky said, her eyes growing wide. "That's a good point, Vi!" She paused to think for a moment, her mind **spinning**.

Violet and the others looked **confused**, but Nicky explained. "Maybe it **wasn't** a student," she began, scratching her snout thoughtfully. Finally, the events of the last few days were starting to make sense!

Nicky continued, "The morning of the project selection, I spotted a **mysterious**

rodent down at the docks who I had never seen before. He was here at Mouseford later that morning, too. And here's the tricky part — he looked like he was PLOTTING with Ruby!"

Nicky went on, watching her friends' reactions. "That same mouse showed up again this morning. He was the one who

A mysterious rodent . . .

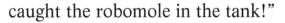

caught the robomole in the tank!"

"I saw him, too!" Violet recalled. "He seemed awfully worried about **protecting** Ruby's island. Did you notice that?"

Paulina nodded, but she also had her own suspicions to add. "Ruby has been acting especially **weird** ever since she presented her project. It seems like she doesn't even know what her invention does. And that doesn't make sense, because it's a **COMPLICATED** project. She must have worked on it for ages!"

"And what about that strange green headband she's been wearing?" Colette noted thoughtfully. "It's not her usual **high-fashion** style. I can't imagine she would have picked that out herself."

Nicky nodded. "So the question is, where did she get it?"

The mice turned to check out what Ruby was up to right at that moment. They saw her fiddling with the little windmill on her island. When the piece broke off in her hand, she turned red and THREW it over her shoulder. It looked like she was just hoping no one would notice!

Oops!

Pam summed up what everyone was thinking. "Something awfully strange is going on. We need to find that **mysterious rodent** and ask him why he's here — and there's no time to lose!"

"You're right, Pam. In fact, the judges should be here any minute," Violet said urgently, checking her watch. "I have an idea! Let's split up. Two of us can go look for the mystery mouse, and the others can stay here to help out with the competition — and to **KEEP AN EYE** on Ruby."

The rest of the Thea Sisters nodded. This was their chance to get to the bottom of the **MYSTERY**. They had to act fast!

Paulina turned to Nicky. "Are you up for it? Let's go find that mouse!"

"Let's do it!" Nicky replied with **DETERMINATION**. "The sooner we find the mysterious rodent, the sooner we'll have some answers!"

Colette was focused on Ruby's headband, which was lying on a table in Ruby's booth. She decided to walk over and take a **closer** look.

"What a **cute** headband! Can I try it on?" Colette asked innocently. She reached out to grab it, but Ruby snatched it from her paw and put it back on her head.

"**PAWS OFF!**" she snapped. "It's delicate!"

CAUGHT in THE ACT

It was time for the final round of the competition to begin. Headmaster de Mousus escorted the five world-famouse scientists who made up the judging panel into the gym, along with the striking Rebecca Flashyfur, who claimed that she was there to observe the competition.

The students murmured excitedly as the jury walked over to the first team. The students from Snoutshire had created the Spectacular Sunnyside Shade, a glow-in-the-dark window shade. It was designed to absorb the sun's rays during the day and release the light at night.

The team pulled down the window shade

and turned off the lights. Everyone blinked while their eyes adjusted. But once the room was **dark**, the shade's glow was more like a weak GLIMMER. It didn't seem to have absorbed much light at all!

"Um . . ." the Snoutshire team captain, Ferguson, guessed in a meek voice, "maybe it needs more time to CHARGE?"

The rest of his teammates shrugged, looking befuddled.

The judges shook their snouts and moved on to the next project.

The team from Mousesala Academy presented their Perfect-Peel Peeler. "It can peel any ingredient in one second or less!" they boasted.

MOUSESALA ACADEMY INVENTION

BEFORE

AFTER

The judges tried the spidery-looking device with a POTATO. But the Perfect-Peel Peeler peeled the potato skin and kept on peeling! Once it was done, all that remained

was a potato the size of a **peanut**. The judges looked at one another, scratching their snouts.

Even the team from Yoshimune Academy had **problems**. They had invented a strong fertilizer that helped plants grow really fast, called Go, Go, Grow! They demonstrated how it was supposed to work with a young lemon plant. The lemons grew big nice and quick, and the judges' eyes grew big, too . . . but then the lemons ROTTED immediately! Holey cheese — the team's presentation had gone totally SOUR!

Ruby's presentation was next, and she was determined not to make a FOOL of herself like the last time. She adjusted her headband, stepped up in front of the judges, and declared confidently, "This is a self-sufficient floating eco-island."

But as soon as Ruby began speaking, Paulina heard a strange murmur coming from the HALLWAY. She signaled to Nicky, and together they headed for a CLOSED DOOR just outside the gym. From there, they heard a male mouse's voice loud and clear, beyond the door.

"The island uses water currents . . ." they heard him say.

Paulina gasped and threw open the door. At last! It was the **mysterious rodent** — just the mouse they were looking for!

Self-sufficient floating eco-island . . .

The rodent was wearing a green headband just like Ruby's, but it had a microphone attachment. When he saw the two mice glaring at him, he jumped in surprise. "Squeak!"

A second later, Nicky and Paulina heard Ruby in the gym. "The island uses water currents Squeak!"

The mouse had been caught in the act! He was telling Ruby what to say through her headband!

He didn't waste a minute before he scurried off down the hall. But Nicky was faster! In no time, she caught up and tackled him to the ground. Paulina POUNCED and helped keep him still.

"I-I can explain!" he yelped.

"I-I can explain!" **echoed** Ruby in the gym, to the confused judges.

THE REAL GENIUS

The mysterious rodent was no longer a mystery. He quickly **confessed** to Nicky and Paulina, and the friends explained to him that the best thing to do was to tell everyone the truth.

The rodent agreed, and the three went back into the gym to find Ruby still stammering to the judges.

"Attention, everyone," Paulina called out. "This is Professor Mouserstein. He's an engineer, and the real inventor of Ruby's island!"

"What?!" exclaimed Headmaster de Mousus. "**WHAT IS GOING ON HERE?**"

"It's true," admitted the engineer in a soft

Time to confess!

voice. He was embarrassed, but also seemed relieved to not have to lie anymore. "I've been working on this project for **yeaRs**. But I didn't have the funding to continue my research, so —"

"So you sold it to Ruby Flashyfur so that she could **cheat** in the competition!" the president of the jury said in disgust.

"No!" exclaimed Mouserstein. "This invention will make a great **contribution** to the field of agriculture. I don't care if people think Ruby invented it or know I did,

just as long as it can be completed."

Ruby's snout turned as red as the sauce on a fresh EXTRA-CHEESE PIZZA, but she didn't say a word.

Headmaster de Mousus stared at his student with sad eyes. "What do you have to say for yourself, Ruby? This is a very SERIOUS matter, and it will have very **serious** consequences."

Rebecca Flashyfur jumped to her daughter's defense. "This fool can't prove anything! I'm calling my **LAWYERS**," she growled.

The Thea Sisters shared a worried look. They knew Ruby had done something wrong, but they didn't want her to be expelled.

From out of the crowd, Ryder appeared

What do you have to say for yourself?

suddenly by his sister's side. "Come on, Ruby," he said loudly so everyone could hear him. "You don't have to lie anymore."

Ruby glared at her brother. What was he DOING?

"Don't take all the blame," he insisted.

"It's time we confessed our secret!"

A CONVINCING CONFESSION

Every mouse held his ~~breath~~, waiting for Ryder to spill his big **SECRET**. Everyone was completely silent. The room was as tense as a mouse at a cat carnival!

What?

"Ruby and I were plotting, it's true," Ryder said to the headmaster, peering down at his paws. "But it was only against our mother!"

Rodents around the room squeaked in surprise, but no one seemed more astonished than Rebecca Flashyfur.

She shot an **ICY-COLD** look at her son. "What in the world are you talking about?" she whispered.

Ruby didn't understand, either, but a **comforting** paw squeeze from her brother reassured her that he knew what he was doing. She just nodded and went along with his plan.

"We know how much you care about **SCIENTIFIC PROGRESS**," Ryder said to his mother. "But you only want to invest in projects with the *greatest* potential."

Rebecca was about to argue that she didn't care one **cat lick** about science, but stopped when she realized that the famouse scientists in the gym were watching admiringly. This wasn't the place for that kind of **CONFESSION**!

At that point, Ryder turned to face the judging panel. "My sister and I believed that Professor Mouserstein's project was obviously exceptional, but we needed to convince our mother."

"That young mouse is smarter than he lets on," Professor Plié whispered to Professor Plotfur, catching on to Ryder's plan. She raised an eyebrow.

Professor Plotfur smiled. "And he has quite a talent for acting, too. I'll have to

We believe in this project . . .

make sure he auditions for my next show!"

Ruby and Rebecca were catching on to Ryder's plan, too, and they both started **playing along**.

"Of course! That's why I decided to participate in the Mice in Science competition with Professor Mouserstein's project in the first place," Ruby confirmed, giving the headmaster a SPARKLING SMILE. "I hoped that Mother would see how important it was and give it her full funding!"

"And then you would get first place in the competition," said Sloane INDIGNANTLY, crossing her arms.

"Oh, but I wouldn't have actually let Ruby compete," Rebecca said confidently, shaking her snout. "I insist on being the only one to finance any projects that I'm involved with. I would **never** have let Ruby accept the prize! You have to understand that."

"Exactly!" Ryder concluded with a smile. "In fact, our mother has decided to finance Professor Mouserstein's research for the NEXT TEN YEARS!"

Rebecca went whiter than a slice of provolone. She was planning on giving a small donation to get her family out of this mess, but now she was stuck paying

Grrr!

That's fabumouse!

for **ten years** of expensive research!

The headmaster paused to think about Ryder's version of the day's events. He twirled his tail and paced on his paws. No matter what, Headmaster de Mousus had to protect the **integrity** of the competition. Mouseford Academy's whole reputation was at stake!

I have a suggestion . . .

Seeing that the headmaster was having trouble making a decision, Professor Rattcliff stepped forward with a solution in the nick of time. "I propose we remove Professor Mouserstein's project from the competition. This contest is for students only. And besides, the island has already received full funding from the generous Mrs. Flashyfur. With the island out of the running, Mouseford Academy will be **out of the competition entirely**."

The headmaster agreed, but added that a board of professors would be meeting to determine a suitable punishment for Ryder and Ruby Flashyfur. After all, whatever their intentions, they had deceived the judges. With that, **the competition could resume!**

THE FABU-FLOP

The Mousekapov Academy students demonstrated their robomole to the judging panel. This time, Valentina the robomole performed perfectly. The judges noted that the robot mole was very useful for finding water — and she was a lot of fun, too!

And finally, Ratridge Academy was up. They had kept their towering project secret by shielding it with a series of cardboard screens and covering it with a thick tarp.

"We have invented . . . the revolutionary **FABU-FUR BOOTH**!"

Sloane, the spokesmouse

for the group, proclaimed. "It can wash, groom, and style fur in just a few minutes!"

Her team removed the screens and tarp, revealing a booth full of brushes, rollers, and wheels.

"Watch this demonstration," Sloane said proudly. "I'll come out of the Fabu-fur refreshed and more **fabumouse** than ever!"

Sloane removed her jumpsuit so that she was wearing just a bathing suit, and went into the machine. Her teammates turned it on and the booth whirred, dinged, and clattered.

VRRRRRRRR!

After three minutes, an alarm chimed and the machine turned off.

Sloane emerged in a cloud of steam. It looked like she'd been through a car wash!

"She's cleaner, but certainly not prettier..." Colette remarked sympathetically. "She's a MESS!"

In two shakes of a mouse's tail, Colette rushed over to Sloane with her stash of natural beauty oils, creams, and powders, and fixed her right up.

"Amazing!" Sloane said of Colette's *touch-ups*.

"Nothing special here, my dear!" Colette confided in her. "Beauty comes naturally —

not from a machine!"

COLETTE'S TOUCH-UPS

BEFORE   AFTER

WE HAVE A WINNER!

It didn't take long before the judges were ready to announce their **FINAL DECISION**. The head of the panel, Professor Mousing from Maussedorf Polytechnic, declared, "The winning project is . . ."

The crowd held its breath. Not a whisker moved.

"**Valentina the robomole** from Mousekapov Academy!"

Thundering applause filled the room as the Mousekapov team celebrated with hugs and high fives. After a moment, Irina, Vladimouse, and Igor jumped up on a table and spoke to the audience as if from a stage.

"We are indebted to Violet from

Mouseford Academy," Irina bellowed. "She helped us through **EVERY STEP** in this competition, and we wouldn't have won without her. In fact, without her, our project probably would have been lost forever! In her honor, the robomole will now be called . . . **Violet Valentina!**"

For the competition's closing ceremonies, the FINE ARTS professors had organized a performance celebrating science. Some of

the students acted in **funny skits** about physics. Professor Aria's students sang **songs** about the lives of famouse inventors. Zoe, Connie, and Alicia performed their Milky Way Mice dance, delighting Professor Plié.

After the show, the students all exchanged email addresses. The Thea Sisters were thrilled to have made so many new friends.

At one point, Pam and Shen took the Mousepod 3000 out of the garage where they had stored it after pulling it out of the bushes. Professor Mouserstein took a look and offered some advice on how to REPAIR it.

The Flashyfurs were the only ones who didn't seem to enjoy the party. Ruby kept her eyes down, and Rebecca silently fumed. *Is she going to be in a terrible mood for the next* ten years? Ruby wondered. Ryder, though, seemed perfectly happy and relaxed.

"Maybe Ryder's the REAL GENIUS . . ." Violet remarked thoughtfully. "He saved his sister from being expelled and got his mother to fund Professor Mouserstein's important projects for ten years!"

"Yup," Paulina agreed with a wink. "I'd say the competition was a SUCCESS after all!"

"And we have a goal for next year's competition, mouselets! We have to get working on the Mousepod . . . 4000!" Pamela joined her closest friends and gave them all an

Don't miss any of these Mouseford Academy adventures!

#1 Drama at Mouseford

#2 The Missing Diary

#3 Mouselets in Danger

#4 Dance Challenge

#5 The Secret Invention

#6 A Mouseford Musical

Don't miss these exciting Thea Sisters adventures!

Thea Stilton and the
Dragon's Code

Thea Stilton and the
Mountain of Fire

Thea Stilton and the
Ghost of the Shipwreck

Thea Stilton and the
Secret City

Thea Stilton and the
Mystery in Paris

Thea Stilton and the
Cherry Blossom Adventure

Thea Stilton and the
Star Castaways

Thea Stilton: Big Trouble
in the Big Apple

Thea Stilton and the
Ice Treasure

Thea Stilton and the
Secret of the Old Castle

Thea Stilton and the
Blue Scarab Hunt

Thea Stilton and the
Prince's Emerald

Thea Stilton and the Mystery
on the Orient Express

Thea Stilton and the
Dancing Shadows

Thea Stilton and the
Legend of the Fire Flowers

Thea Stilton and the
Spanish Dance Mission

Thea Stilton and the
Journey to the Lion's Den

Thea Stilton and the
Great Tulip Heist

Thea Stilton and the
Chocolate Sabotage

Thea Stilton and the
Missing Myth

Thea Stilton and the
Lost Letters

Be sure to read all my fabumouse adventures!

#1 Lost Treasure of the Emerald Eye

#2 The Curse of the Cheese Pyramid

#3 Cat and Mouse in a Haunted House

#4 I'm Too Fond of My Fur!

#5 Four Mice Deep in the Jungle

#6 Paws Off, Cheddarface!

#7 Red Pizzas for a Blue Count

#8 Attack of the Bandit Cats

#9 A Fabumouse Vacation for Geronimo

#10 All Because of a Cup of Coffee

#11 It's Halloween, You 'Fraidy Mouse!

#12 Merry Christmas, Geronimo!

#13 The Phantom of the Subway

#14 The Temple of the Ruby of Fire

#15 The Mona Mousa Code

#16 A Cheese-Colored Camper

#17 Watch Your Whiskers, Stilton!

#18 Shipwreck on the Pirate Islands

#19 My Name Is Stilton, Geronimo Stilton

#20 Surf's Up, Geronimo!

#21 The Wild, Wild West

#22 The Secret of Cacklefur Castle

A Christmas Tale

#23 Valentine's Day Disaster

#24 Field Trip to Niagara Falls

#25 The Search for Sunken Treasure

#26 The Mummy with No Name

#27 The Christmas Toy Factory

#28 Wedding Crasher

#29 Down and Out Down Under

#30 The Mouse Island Marathon

#31 The Mysterious Cheese Thief

Christmas Catastrophe

#32 Valley of the Giant Skeletons

#33 Geronimo and the Gold Medal Mystery

#34 Geronimo Stilton, Secret Agent

#35 A Very Merry Christmas

#36 Geronimo's Valentine

#37 The Race Across America

#38 A Fabumouse School Adventure

#39 Singing Sensation

#40 The Karate Mouse

#41 Mighty Mount Kilimanjaro

#42 The Peculiar Pumpkin Thief

#43 I'm Not a Supermouse!

#44 The Giant Diamond Robbery

#45 Save the White Whale!

#46 The Haunted Castle

#47 Run for the Hills, Geronimo!

#48 The Mystery in Venice

#49 The Way of the Samurai

#50 This Hotel Is Haunted!

#51 The Enormouse Pearl Heist

#52 Mouse in Space!

#53 Rumble in the Jungle

#54 Get into Gear, Stilton!

#55 The Golden Statue Plot

#56 Flight of the Red Bandit

The Hunt for the Golden Book

#57 The Stinky Cheese Vacation

#58 The Super Chef Contest

#59 Welcome to Moldy Manor

The Hunt for the Curious Cheese

#60 The Treasure of Easter Island

Don't miss my journeys through time!

Be sure to read all of our magical special edition adventures!

THE KINGDOM OF FANTASY

THE QUEST FOR PARADISE:
THE RETURN TO THE KINGDOM OF FANTASY

THE AMAZING VOYAGE:
THE THIRD ADVENTURE IN THE KINGDOM OF FANTASY

THE DRAGON PROPHECY:
THE FOURTH ADVENTURE IN THE KINGDOM OF FANTASY

THE VOLCANO OF FIRE:
THE FIFTH ADVENTURE IN THE KINGDOM OF FANTASY

THE SEARCH FOR TREASURE:
THE SIXTH ADVENTURE IN THE KINGDOM OF FANTASY

THE ENCHANTED CHARMS:
THE SEVENTH ADVENTURE IN THE KINGDOM OF FANTASY

THEA STILTON: THE JOURNEY TO ATLANTIS

THEA STILTON: THE SECRET OF THE FAIRIES

THEA STILTON: THE SECRET OF THE SNOW

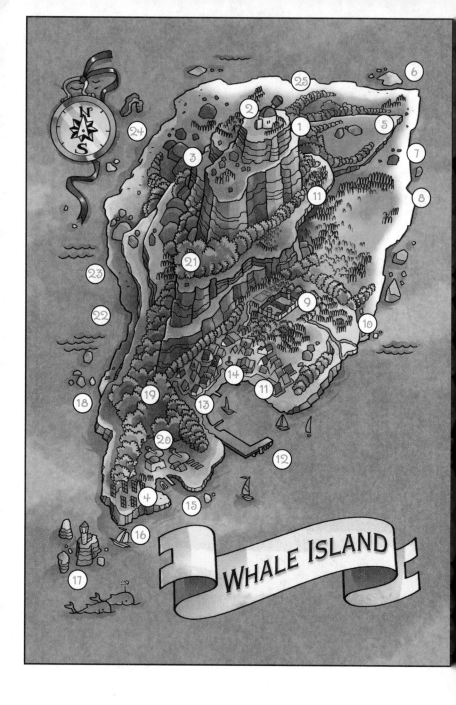

WHALE ISLAND

MAP OF WHALE ISLAND

1. Falcon Peak
2. Observatory
3. Mount Landslide
4. Solar Energy Plant
5. Ram Plain
6. Very Windy Point
7. Turtle Beach
8. Beachy Beach
9. Mouseford Academy
10. Kneecap River
11. Mariner's Inn
12. Port
13. Squid House
14. Town Square
15. Butterfly Bay
16. Mussel Point
17. Lighthouse Cliff
18. Pelican Cliff
19. Nightingale Woods
20. Marine Biology Lab
21. Hawk Woods
22. Windy Grotto
23. Seal Grotto
24. Seagulls Bay
25. Seashell Beach

THANKS FOR READING, AND GOOD-BYE UNTIL OUR NEXT ADVENTURE!

Thea Sisters